Five Little Monkeys
Wash the Car

For Sebi, who LOVES cars!

ISBN 0-439-15075-2

Copyright © 2000 by Eileen Christelow.
All rights reserved.
Published by Scholastic Inc., 555 Broadway, New York, NY 10012,
by arrangement with Clarion Books, a Houghton Mifflin Company imprint.
SCHOLASTIC and associated logos are trademarks and/or
registered trademarks of Scholastic Inc.

12 11 10 9 8 7 6 5 4 3 2   1 2 3 4 5 6/0

Printed in the U.S.A.   08

First Scholastic printing, September 2001

The illustrations were executed in watercolor and pencil.
The text was set in 18-point New Century Schoolbook.

Five Little Monkeys Wash the Car

Eileen Christelow

SCHOLASTIC INC.

New York Toronto London Auckland Sydney
Mexico City New Delhi Hong Kong

The five little monkeys, and Mama, can never drive far in their rickety, rattletrap wreck of a car.

"I've had it!" says Mama. "Let's sell this old heap!" She makes a big sign that says, CAR FOR SALE—CHEAP!

CAR FOR SALE —CHEAP!

Then Mama goes in.
"There's some work I
should do."
"Okay," say the monkeys.
"We have work too!"

"This car is so *icky!*"
"So sticky and slimy!"
"How can we sell
an old car that's so grimy?"

So two little monkeys
spray with a hose,
while three little monkeys
scrub the car till it glows.

"But the car is still rusty!"
"It stinks! Oh, *pee-yew!*"
"No one will buy it."
"What can we do?"

"I KNOW!" says one little monkey.

I KNOW!

7

Then four little monkeys
find paint in the shed.
Blue, yellow, and green,
purple, pink, and bright red.

They paint the old car
with designs all around,
while one little monkey
sprays perfume he found.

9

The five little monkeys
sit down and wait.
But no one comes by—
and it's getting late!

I KNOW!

"The car looks terrific!"
"It smells so good too!"
"Maybe no one can see it here."
"What should we do?"

"I KNOW!" says one little monkey.

So three little monkeys
start pushing the car.
The monkey who's steering
can't see very far.

Then one little monkey
shouts, "Park it right here!
Wait! It's rolling too fast!
Can't you stop? Can't you steer?"

The monkey who's steering
can't reach the brake.
The car rolls downhill to the . . .

. . . BROWN SWAMPY LAKE!

"Well, now we're in trouble!"
"We're stuck in this goo!"
"We'll never get out."
"Oh, what can we do?"

"WE KNOW!" rumbles a voice from the swamp.

WE KNOW!

"The **CROCODILES!**"
five little monkeys all shout.
One crocodile says,
"*We'll* help you get out!"

More crocodiles rise
from the wet swampy goo.
"We'll push this old car.
But YOU must push too."

The monkeys all quake.
"What they say isn't true!"
"They'll eat us for supper!"
"Oh, what can we do?"

"I KNOW!" says one little monkey.

"Oh, crocodiles!" she calls,
"I heard you were strong!
But if you need *our* help,
I must have heard wrong."

"We're strong!" roar the crocs.
"We're the strongest by far!
And we can push anything
—even a car!"

So they puff and they pant
till they look very ill.
But they push that old car
to the top of the hill.

Then one monkey whispers,
"We're *still* in a stew!
If they don't go home now,
what can we do?"

"I KNOW!" says one little monkey.

23

"Poor crocs!" say the monkeys.
"How tired you are!
You'll never walk home!
What you need is a . . .

...CAR!"

The crocodiles buy it.
They pay with a check,
then climb right inside.
"We can use this old wreck!"

The monkeys all run
to tell Mama their tale.
"You might have been eaten!"
(She's turning quite pale.)

"We know!" say the monkeys.
"We're lucky, it's true.
But we *did* sell the car . . .
Can we buy one that's new?"

The five little monkeys
and Mama go shop
for a fancy new car—
with a convertible top!

And the crocodiles?
They really like their old heap.
It's such a fine car
for a long summer's . . .

...SLEEP!